Then Came Christmas

A short story sequel to March to November

Byddi Lee

DEDICATION

For the people with empty chairs at their table at
Christmas

ACKNOWLEDGEMENTS

Thanks to the Potluck Publishers for their critiquing, support and suggestions. To my writing buddies for journeying with me and understanding the rollercoaster that the creative life has been, especially this past few years, you are my tribe. Huge thanks to my family and friends for their unwavering faith in me and for giving me the courage to keep writing.

December 20th

The young boy's voice hit the high notes, like
sunshine on a snowy morning, crisp, clear and heart-
achingly beautiful. Tracey swallowed a lump in her
throat and tilted her head back, trying to contain the
tears behind her eyelids. "O Holy Night" always had
that effect on her. It had been one of Molly's
favourites too. Tracey reigned in her emotions and
joined in the applause as the boy bowed. She felt a dig
in her ribs.

"The twins are on next," Carla whispered in her
ear.

The stage lights dimmed as the curtains pulled
closed. A few clunky bangs and the scrape of heavy
furniture along wooden floorboards could be heard
above the fidget and murmur of the audience. The
spotlight lit up the curtains, and the fizz in the crowd
settled.

Tracey watched her friend's reaction to the performance. Carla's tweedy green eyes sparkled with love and pride as she gazed up at her sons on stage. She'd tucked her shoulder-length auburn hair behind her ears. The ends poked out, framing her jaw-line. Carla's head dipped in time with the music as the boys scraped out "Silent Night" on their violins. The skin between her eyebrows pulled into a tight little wrinkle, and a nervous smile transformed into lip nibbling as one of the boys hit a bum note. Carla's features relaxed as the musicians battled on and regained their stride. By the end of the carol, her face was a rapture of pride and relief.

Tracey gave Carla's arm a squeeze. "They were really good," Tracey said, relieved that she could say so truthfully.

"I wish Mickey had been able to come," Carla said as the assembly hall lights came on. They shuffled out, spilling into the clangour of chat and excited greetings in the lobby. The Christmas tree lights sparkled. Glitter winked and glinted at them where the children's artwork and card-making were on display.

"It's not really his scene, is it?" Tracey said.

"Yeah, but he is their dad," Carla answered grumpily. "I wanted him to see that all that cat-torture noise had amounted to something. Jesus, he complains enough about the noise they make practising. It's better than the noise they make fighting, not that he's around much to hear that. It's all work, work, work with him."

"I know, but don't be too hard on him," Tracey said, looking around her. "There are very few daddies here. Could you imagine our daddies going to stuff like this?"

Carla laughed. "Some chance. Unless you opened a bar at the back–" She looked at Tracey and sucked in air between her teeth. "Sorry."

"Nah, forget it," Tracey said. She was over feeling sorry for herself for having had an alcoholic father who drank himself to death. "Look, there's tea." She pointed to a long table. A huge silver kettle held the hot water on one end, and a giant teapot sat beside it, brewing a strong cuppa. A couple of dozen cups sat in saucers beside it, and further down, platters of tray bakes made Tracey's mouth water. "The school always puts on a lovely spread." She nibbled on the edge of a caramel square. Its creamy sweetness burst on her tongue and blossomed in her mouth. "I'm glad Mickey doesn't come, and I get the spare ticket."

Carla rolled her eyes and shook her head.

"So, what do you guys have planned for Christmas?" Tracey asked as they lined up.

"We're just keeping it a simple family affair," Carla said, balancing the cup, saucer and a plate in her right hand as she picked up serving tongs in her left. "We'll do Mass on Christmas Eve and then take it easy on Christmas morning. The boys like to stay at home to play with their presents, and then Mum, Dad and Mickey's parents will come over for dinner about three. You?"

Simple…family…

Tracey felt a pang of envy and sorrow. Her family didn't do simple. If, by some miracle, everyone agreed to come together, there'd probably be world-war-three.

"There's only Mum and Dermot and Cara left in Belfast. Everyone else is abroad or…" She didn't want to admit that she had a brother in jail. She pretended to look for something on the table in front of her before adding, "We...we haven't decided yet." She picked up a cup of steaming hot tea. "I need to discuss it with Tommy."

"Well, you'd need to get a move on. It's only five days away," Carla said, helping herself to a huge cherry scone slathered in butter. She lifted half the scone and offered to put it on Tracey's plate.

Anxiety coiled in Tracey's gut. She waved the scone away. Her appetite had evaporated.

December 21st

Tracey watched Dermot move stiffly towards the
bassinet, stooped and diminished compared to the
dashing, handsome brother she was used to. His
usually shiny raven-black hair looked dull and needed
a cut. His skin was pallid from lack of sleep and his
dark eyes sunken from the stresses of being a single
parent. No more the trendy heartthrob, Dermot
slouched around in jogging bottoms and spew stained
sweatshirts.

It still felt weird for Tracey to meet him in the
apartment of the woman he'd left Molly for. Molly's
will was still not settled. Technically, when she had
died, she was still Dermot's wife as she'd not begun
the divorce proceedings yet, but they had made a
financial separation. She'd taken over the marital
home with help from her dad, so it would probably
go to her parents. It was a battle Dermot said he had
no heart for. He'd told Tracey that he didn't want to

move back to his old house. It didn't feel right to bring Cara to live there after Molly had died, and Sheila's apartment was empty.

"When Sheila recovers, she'll come back, and we'll be a family," Dermot would say.

He was being unrealistic. Even though the doctors were pleased with how well he was healing, Tracey could tell he was still in a lot of physical and emotional pain. Two days after Molly, his ex-wife, had died falling from a window, Dermot's girlfriend and new-mother of his child had developed postpartum psychosis and tried the kill the baby. Dermot had stepped in to save his daughter but had been badly scalded by boiling water in the process. Sheila had been in a secure psychiatric unit ever since.

Tracey stood up to lift the baby from his arms. Cara was bundled up in white fleecy wool-texture baby-grow that had lamb's ears with velvety pink insides poking out of a little hood. Across the front, it said, "I'm the Baaa…." Tracey had bought it for her soon after Cara was born, but it only fit her properly now, seven weeks later. Dermot was good about dressing Cara up in the little outfits Tracey was constantly buying.

Tracey's heart swelled as she gazed upon her sleeping niece, taking in the smooth skin, the little button nose and the perfect rosebud lips. She squeezed her. Cara wriggled and waved a fist but didn't wake up. Tracey kissed her forehead and inhaled her sweet aroma.

"So, how did your visit with Sheila go?" Tracey asked her brother, tearing her eyes away from Cara's face.

Dermot sighed. He touched his daughter's hand.

Her tiny fingers wrapped themselves around his like a little monkey grip. His features lightened. He swallowed, and his eyes flooded with gloom. "Sheila refused to see me. The doctors say that if she doesn't want to see me, they can't make her."

"Is it because you're not family or not married?" Tracey asked, rocking Cara, enjoying the warmth and weight in her arms.

"No, she just gets too upset," Dermot answered. He took his finger back and sat down on the cream sofa.

Tracey sat beside him.

"I just… it's just." Dermot sighed heavily and sat forward, putting his elbows on his knees and forehead into his hands. "She refuses to see her own daughter."

"She's ill. You know that."

"I know, but it's just so sad. It's Cara's first Christmas…" He looked at Tracey with sad chocolate eyes, soaked with fatigue and despair. "Will I see you on Christmas Day?"

"Of course you will." Tracey would have hugged her poor broken brother if her arms weren't full of his daughter. "We always do Christmas Day together."

"When?" Dermot asked, his dark features lifted. "When's dinner?"

Tracey stiffened. "I don't know, Dermot." She couldn't make eye contact. "I'm not sure exactly what we're doing yet. I need to talk to Tommy."

"I see," Dermot said. His shoulders sagged, and he sighed heavily. "I've tried to talk to Tommy about the whole Molly thing…"

The mention of her best friend's name drove a shard of glass through her chest. Tracey couldn't talk about it, so she couldn't blame Tommy for avoiding Dermot either. Molly had been like a sister to him. It was too soon. The pain still burned white-hot.

"I…We…Don't…" She didn't know what she could say without making the relationship between him and her boyfriend, Tommy, worse.

"I didn't mean for any of this to happen," Dermot said, his voice hoarse and raspy. "I thought Molly would get over it. I never imagined that she'd…You know how God-awful-sorry I am."

Tracey felt a rush of anger at his naivety. He needed to give Tommy time to work through his grief and anger. It didn't help that Tommy believed that Molly had flung herself to her death and not fallen by accident. Tracey clung to the idea that Molly would never kill herself. She'd promised Tracey as much, but Tommy blamed Dermot for Molly's death, simple as that.

Except, it wasn't simple – Tracey loved both her boyfriend and her brother. It was family. It was complicated.

"I'll see about Christmas Dinner…I'll do my best," she said but couldn't bear the hope that flared in his tired eyes.

December 22nd

Tracey stepped back to admire her work. The bow window in the living room was filled with a white tree decked out with blue and silver decorations. The windows, black with the night outside, reflected three Traceys surrounded by a mini forest of white gleaming trees. Her blond hair, winter-pale skin and white shirt made her look shiny yet topped with gold. Tracey loved how the tree looked. She had wanted something that did not remind her of the real tree that Molly had put up every year. Molly's tree had always been decked out in different kinds of ornaments all the way back to Molly's childhood, some hand-made, others gifts or souvenirs. Everything Molly hung on her tree had had a story, and Tracey loved hearing those stories as they decorated the tree together.

This year there'd be no stories, no Molly. Thinking about it brought on that ache in her chest that was all too familiar now. Missing Molly weighed so heavy on her some days, she wondered how she got out of bed and on with life. And Christmas – oh God – how do you get through Christmas dragging that grief with you through the chirpy holiday greetings and the endless partying? Tracey had contemplated no tree, but it was her first Christmas with Tommy. He too missed Molly, his cousin who had been more like a sister to him. They needed a new way to do Christmas, starting with a fake white tree.

Empty boxes filled the coffee table sitting between the couch and the fireplace. Along the mantel shelf, Tracey had arranged eight-inch tall, white wooden letters that spelt "Peace" set into a board. Each wooden letter had carved figurines attached to them around the base. Some were shepherds, others angels, and below the "A" a babe in a manger with his parents on either side. Tracey felt satisfied she'd honoured the religious aspect of the occasion, and yet it still looked elegant. Below that, she'd hung a lush, fluffy white tinsel garland from the mantel shelf.

"It looks beautiful, darling," Tommy said, putting his arm around her waist. "As do you." He kissed her forehead.

"You're pretty gorgeous yourself." Tracey looked at him and tried to take a mental picture of that moment. Tommy, a professional hairstylist, showcased his colleague's work with a great head of dark blond hair cut short at the back and sides with some length and "choppiness," as he called it, on top. She gazed into his grey eyes, set above high cheekbones, balanced by a square jaw. Gorgeous, she thought, no other way to describe it.

"Are we done here?" he asked, his voice husky in

her ear.

"One last thing." She placed three large white candles and three blue candles of varying sizes in the grate of the fireplace. Using bundles of white tinsel, she arranged a frothy cloud beneath the grate, so it popped out around the base of the candles, disguising the ugly brickwork and heat-pocked metal of the grate. They'd never used this fireplace.

"We should try and get that working," she said, tidying up the jumble of boxes before her.

"It might be obstructed," Tommy said. "I could look into it. Right enough…" He came up behind her and hugged her. "It would be nice to sit in front of it on a cold Christmas evening and let it warm us up."

"Mentioning Christmas," Tracey said as Tommy nuzzled her neck, sending a cascade of tingles skittering across her skin. "We need to talk."

Tommy stopped, and Tracey immediately wished she'd kept her mouth shut.

"I agree," he said, taking her hand and guiding her around the coffee table to the sofa to sit down. "Dad has been asking us if we would join him and Aunty Aileen and Uncle Ben for Christmas Eve dinner."

Tracey groaned. Molly's mother could be difficult. She'd brow-beaten Molly all her life. Now Molly was dead, the woman hated Dermot. That was her prerogative, but Aileen never missed the opportunity to take a dig at Tracey's brother. It was hard work and not how Tracey wanted to spend Christmas Eve.

"Please?" He kissed her nose. "Molly and Dermot used to go every year. It would really help them get through this year if we went."

"Well…" Tracey said, knowing that if she said no, she'd feel shitty about it, but …maybe it could work in her favour. "If we do that, can we have my Mum and Dermot and Cara over for Christmas dinner?"

Tommy froze.

"I know it's a big ask," she continued in a rush. "But you promised you'd try to move on with Dermot, and it's Cara's first Christmas. I know you enjoy us looking after Cara every Thursday. You do love that wee baby, and I've always—"

"No."

"No? Like, just no? No negotiation?" Tracey fought to push down her anger and not let it get the better of her. The injustice of it. That she was prepared to put up with the vicious sniping from Aunty Aileen, yet Tommy was not prepared to even discuss meeting her halfway, was too much. Tracey stood up, lifted the empty boxes she'd stacked into one another, carried them to the corner of the room, opened the little door to the under-stairs storage area, and flung the boxes to the back of the cupboard. She closed the door hard, half intending to slam it but pulled back at the last second. It still made a bang loud enough to make their giant black and white Great Dane-sized mongrel cower in the corner and whimper.

"It's okay, Wolfie," Tracey said and reined in her fury as best she could before facing the man she loved.

Tommy stood with his head cocked to one side, his forehead in furrows of wrinkled skin and his hands on his hips.

"Ah, don't be like that," he said. "I'm sorry." He held out a hand to her.

She looked at it. Anger burned her throat, but her eyes filled with tears. She wasn't angry at him. She understood why he had an issue with Dermot. Her brother had been a total shit to Molly. Even though Tracey believed that Molly had not committed suicide, Dermot's behaviour ruined the final few months of Molly's life. Yes, Tracey was angry with Dermot, but she was mad at Molly for dying and leaving her, livid at Sheila for... oh Christ, where to start with that?

Tracey's hand trembled as she reached for Tommy's. He pulled her into a hug, and she pressed her cheek against the soft jersey fabric and listened to the thud of his heart. The first sob broke over her like a wave crashing on rocks. She stopped fighting back the tears and gave in to crying. Tommy rocked her gently, rubbed her back and murmured, "It's okay, honey," and, "Let it all out. I've got you." Wolfie pressed against her legs, and she felt the thwack of his tail.

"I miss Molly too," Tracey finally said. "But I also miss Dermot. I just want you two not to hate each other." She shook her head as she scratched Wolfie behind the ears. "And there's Cara. I don't want to miss her first Christmas. She's innocent in all this."

"I don't mind having your mum here for Christmas dinner," Tommy said. "And Cara, well, she's too young to notice. But please. I can't face Dermot. I'm afraid I'll punch him."

"And I won't punch Aunty Aileen?"

"Actually, that would be something to see," he said with a grin and tousled her hair.

Tracey rolled her eyes but didn't have a smile to go with it. "I guess I'll call over to Tommy on Christmas evening after we have dinner. Maybe I'll take Mum with me to see Dermot and Cara too."

"Will I tell Dad to come for Christmas Dinner, and we can forget about Christmas Eve with Molly's parents?" Tommy asked.

Tracey shook her head. No point in being petty. "No, it's okay. We'll do Christmas Eve with him and Molly's parents. What does he usually do on Christmas Day?" Maybe she'd work on that as a bargaining chip tomorrow.

"I don't know," Tommy said. "This is the first year we've been friends since I left for London... since Mum died. I've never asked him."

At least that's one relationship patched up, Tracey thought. Maybe next year they'd celebrate with Dermot and Cara. But how the hell was she going to break the news about this year to Dermot?

December 23rd

Tracey thought she'd misheard Orla when she'd said she would call round to her house at ten that morning so they could go for a run on the towpath.

A run? Orla?

Tommy said that hell might freeze over and as it turned out, overnight, it almost had. When they'd woken up that morning, all the trees were frosted. Blades of grass and fallen leaves snapped underfoot as Tracey supervised Wolfie's ablutions in the front garden. The big dog snuffled about and found a spot between the privet hedge and the wooden gate as if he was seeking privacy. A hard job for a dog his size in the postage-stamp-garden they had.

He sauntered back to Tracey, head held high, didn't stop, but instead headed straight back into the warm house. Tracey held her breath, followed the steam cloud, and cleaned up after him before following him indoors.

Inside, one of the mirror balls caught the morning sun shining in through the bay window and threw a hundred discs of light onto the walls and ceiling of the living room.

"Tommy, look," Tracey cried in delight. "It's gorgeous."

Tommy came through from the kitchen with cups of coffee, smiling like a big kid.

"That's brilliant." He handed Tracey her coffee and set his own down. He went to the tree and gently spun the mirror. The reflected circles spun around the room.

Wolfie barked and jumped up, trying to catch them as they swung past the wall in front of him. He made an awful racket.

"Okay, okay," Tracy said. "Enough with the 'Ballroom of Romance'."

"I was thinking more of our old discos, but if you wanna go that far back." Tommy took the cup he'd just given her, set it beside his and held her as they waltzed around the room. Wolfie continued to bark at the spots of lights as they oscillated back to their original positions. They had just finished settling him down when the doorbell rang, and he made a mad dash to the front hall.

"My God," Tracey looked at her watch. "That's Orla, on time, for running? I feel like I'm in an alternate reality. You hold the dog, and I'll slip on out. Love you."

"Love you too." Tommy kissed her. "Have a good one. I'll keep your coffee for later," he called after her.

Orla was dressed for running. Not that she dressed the same as most runners might. She wore bright pink

Nike running shoes covered with bright yellow reflective flashes. Tracey guessed that since these were the most expensive part of her outfit, Orla must have decided they would be the foundation for her colour scheme. Her hair, which was had been dyed fiery red this week, was pulled into a top knot. It contrasted nicely with the fluorescent yellow headband around her forehead. She wore a yellow jacket in the same shade, open to the waist. Her ample bosom, squashed into a tight cerise-pink vest top, spilt over the edges in bulges of pale flesh. Her pink animal print leggings did nothing to help diminish the girth of her hips. She'd be hard to lose on a dark night, Tracey thought.

Orla saw Tracy, clapped her hands together and jogged on the spot. "Okay, are we ready for this?"

"Looks like we are," Tracey said. "Nice outfit. Where did you get those leggings?"

"Internet," Orla said, taking off at a brisk jog down Palestine Street.

Tracey ran up beside her and matched her pace. "So what's the motivation for this? I thought you hated running."

"I do," Orla panted little puffs of steam into the frigid air. "But I've met someone."

"You have?" Tracey said, delighted. "Who is it? Where did you meet him? Are you guys serious?"

"Look," Orla gasped. "I can run…or…" She sucked in a few breaths. "I can talk." She panted again. "Pick one!"

Her face was red. Sweat ran down her temple from her headband. They'd only been running for about three minutes and hadn't even reached the River Lagan yet.

"Talk," Tracey decided. "Talking and a brisk walk

are every bit as good as jogging, you know."

"Really?" Orla stopped, bent over and put her hands on her knees. Her breath billowed and hung in the air around her.

Tracey stopped running and stood a couple of paces ahead of her. Orla had the heart of a lion, but if she kept up running at this pace, in her condition, she'd be likely to have a heart attack, lion or not.

Orla stood up and walked towards Tracey, and they fell in to pace again, this time walking. Oblivious to the traffic clattering across the Ormeau Bridge, the Lagan River flowed smoothly beneath it. The silky water mirrored the frost-kissed trees along the banks, their leafless branches reaching like twisted fingers into a fresh blue sky.

"It's a beautiful morning," Tracey said. "Thanks for making me get out and enjoy it."

They stood still for a minute, breathing mist out of their lungs and watched as a flock of crows lifted from a stand of trees and winged their way towards the docks. The girls walked on.

"So I've met this guy. He's a friend of a friend, and well, he hasn't exactly noticed me yet," Orla said.

Tracey wondered if the guy was blind. Orla was hard to miss. Tracey said nothing, and Orla went on, "And that's good because right now, I want to lose some weight, you know, get in shape."

Tracey's heart wrung with sympathy for her friend.

"Orla, you are beautiful, inside and out. If you feel you need to lose weight, I'll help you, but don't just lose weight for him, do it for yourself."

"Wise words, Kimosabe, but they won't get me laid."

Tracey gently punched her arm and laughed.

"Okay, what do you want to do?"

"Will you come running with me regularly?" Orla asked. "I know you like running, even if I hate it. I worked out how many times I need to run before I can justify having spent such a shit load of money on all this gear."

"So, how many times?" Tracey asked.

"A lot," Orla scrunched her face up and looked fairly disgusted with herself.

"Alright," Tracey said. "Let's do once a week, but we need to talk about diet too. No more binge drinking and Lucozade cures."

"Oops," Orla said. "Too late. I had Lucozade this morning already. Sorry. Let's leave the diet till after Christmas, okay?"

"Okay. What are you doing for Christmas anyway?" Tracey asked. "Are you going down to the country?"

"Yeah. The usual. Going to my Granny's in Armagh. I love it, hanging out with all the aunties and uncles and all us cousins together. It's great. Tons of food, drink and partying, with a bit of bitching thrown in. Pretty perfect, really." Orla's eyes twinkled, and Tracey knew that feisty Orla would love that crazy scene.

"What about you?" Orla asked.

"Oh, Orla," Tracey said. "I feel awful. Dermot has no one to spend Christmas with. I don't know how to tell him. I've agreed to spend Christmas Eve at Aunty Aileen's."

"Oh, God."

"I know, but Molly and Dermot always went, and without Molly, they are going to be so lonely. Usually, I'd take Mum to Molly and Dermot's on Christmas

Day, but Tommy can't bear to do that. I just wish we could try to work this out."

"Tommy is really stubborn – I know that much," Orla said. "It's a tough one."

"So, now I have Mum coming to ours, then I have to take her to Dermot's and leave Tommy by himself–"

"Well, he's a big boy. It's his call," Orla interrupted.

"I know, I know," Tracey said. "But it's the principle of the matter. Dermot has really changed since Cara arrived, and Molly…you know…"

Orla nodded and pressed her lips tight together.

"But Tommy won't even give him a chance," Tracey continued. "All I want for Christmas is a happy family day."

"Good luck with that," Orla grunted. She stopped and put her hand on Tracey's shoulder, "Just tell him straight - you want a Christmas Truce. Jaysus, didn't the Brits and the Germans do it during the war? Didn't they play a game of football with barbed wire goals and all?"

"I didn't realise you were such a history buff."

"I'm not," Orla said. "I saw it on a Christmas song video or a Sainsbury's commercial or something."

"Ha, so it must be true," Tracey said.

"No, really it was," Orla nodded earnestly. "It really happened. It might even have been on the history channel. But the bottom line is, Tracey, you're too nice. You're trying to keep everyone else happy. Tell Tommy what you want and stick to your guns. He'll come round. But what exactly do you want?"

"I just don't want Cara to be looking back years from now and wondering why there's no family pictures of her first Christmas," Tracey said.

"So you want a picture with everyone in it on Cara's first Christmas?" Orla said. "A regular Waltons shot, right?"

Tracey nodded, annoyed at the tears that sprang to her eyes. It seemed so silly and trivial, but it meant so much.

"Well, there's always Photoshop," Orla said.

Tracey snorted and punched her lightly again. "You're a bitch, Orla," she said fondly.

"That's ma job!" Orla said while punching her back.

When Tracey returned home, Tommy was waving off a man Tracey had never seen before.

"Who was that?" she asked.

"A chimney sweep," he replied.

"Really? Can we light the fire now?"

"Not yet. He checked the flue, it's still open, but there may be debris and soot in there that might catch fire. He didn't have time to do it this side of Christmas, but he's coming back before the New Year," Tommy said.

"That's brilliant," Tracey said. Tommy was the sweetest guy, and generally, he gave her anything she wanted, except for this one thing, a family Christmas with Dermot and Cara. And somehow, she wanted that more than anything else. Maybe after they'd suffered through dinner at Aileen's, she'd have more bargaining power. Tracey wasn't taking no for an answer yet.

December 24th

The dinner had been as delicious as it was tense.
Aileen roasted a side of salmon and served scalloped
potatoes and broccolini – a type of broccoli from
Italy, she informed Tracey. It tasted like regular
broccoli with long stems, but Tracey didn't argue with
her. Aileen had the house decked out to the hilt.
Every shelf and tabletop had Christmas ornaments,
and she had three different trees. No wonder Molly
had always gone all out for Christmas. She'd been
used to it. Tracey's mother, Carmel, hadn't bothered
with decorations since her youngest had left home.

They sat around the dining table, finishing off their
dinner. So far, nothing unpleasant had been said.
Aileen had hung back on the cutting remarks, and
Tracey was beginning to think they'd come out of this
evening unscathed.

"That was marvellous, Aileen," Tommy's father,
Sean, said. "I won't need to eat again for a week."

22

"Oh, I'm sure you'll be up for a big turkey dinner tomorrow," Aileen said. "Aren't you going to be spending the day with your lovely big son?" She gazed up at Tommy with innocent eyes.

"We…I…" Tommy ran aground.

"Oh, I'm sorry," Aileen said smoothly. "Do you have other plans, Sean?"

"No, Tommy and I don't usually spend Christmas Day together," Sean said. "It didn't occur to me."

"Ach now, that's just because he's been away in London all those years," Aileen said. "Close family should spend the day together. Don't you think, Tracey?"

"You know Aunty Aileen, I keep telling Tommy that," Tracey said aloud. Interfering bitch, she thought but smiled sweetly back. That blew up her bargaining chip. She couldn't uninvite Sean later if Tommy said no to her asking, once more, if Dermot could join them.

"Well, that's settled then. What time are you eating?" Aileen picked up the empty plates, scraped and stacked them.

"Sean, we'd love to have you. Come over about three, okay?" Tracey said and genuinely meant it.

Sean, his face flushed red, said, "Thanks, I'd love that."

Tracey was glad he could come.

They declined Aileen's offer of a cup of tea and made their excuses to go soon after.

Tommy was driving his dad home. As soon as they pulled out of Aileen's driveway, Sean turned around in the front seat to address Tracey in the back.

"Love, I'm sorry to have put you on the spot about tomorrow. You know how Aileen is," he said.

23

"Seriously, I'll be right on my own."

"Sitting by yerself in the dark?" Tommy said.

Sean looked confused as Tracey and Tommy laughed at the old joke.

"How many Irish mothers does it take to change a light bulb," Tommy said.

"Oh right," Sean said, "Yes, funny, yes. But you know what I mean."

"Look, don't worry," Tracey said. "You're welcome. Really you are."

"Ah, thanks, love." He hesitated and scratched his goatee. "I've no gifts. Is Cara coming?"

"No," Tracey and Tommy said together with noticeably different tones.

"I see," Sean said. "That's a pity. That wane needs her family. Maybe it's time to mend some fences or at least give Dermot the hammer."

"Dad," Tommy said tersely. "Just leave it. We'll see you tomorrow, okay?"

Tracey could have cried. She had hoped to have one last chance at cracking Tommy, but this conversation with his dad had closed the option down completely. They dropped Sean off and drove in silence until they arrived home.

Wolfie greeted them at the front door, ran out into the freezing night, peed quickly and then bounced around as they ushered him into the house. Tommy left the other lights in the room off and switched on the Christmas tree lights. It cast a lovely Christmas glow throughout the room, and Tracey tried not to be annoyed with Tommy for being stubborn about Dermot. There was no point in ruining what she had left of Christmas.

"Let's start our Christmas now," Tommy said. He

bent towards and kissed her. "Our first Christmas."
He kissed her again, this time with more urgency,
then pulled back and lingered, nibbling her lips with
his.

She forced herself to relax and found herself
softening in his embrace.

"Why don't you light the candles." Tommy
nodded at the fireplace. His smile lit up his face. "And
I'll get us some wine."

She nearly had the first candle lit when she heard a
rustle, faint and far away, up the chimney.

"Ho Ho Ho," Tommy called from the backyard.

What the hell was he doing out there?

"Is that sleigh bells I hear?" Tracey thought she
heard him say. Then she heard another rattle from
somewhere up in the chimney and a muffled caw. A
small but heavy black bag landed on one of the
candles. It was attached to a string. Tracey stared at it,
to surprised to move. Then she heard more noises up
the chimney – clicks, thuds and a rustling that grew
louder and louder, until a crow burst out of the
fireplace, right into her face, in a fury of feathers and
soot. She jumped back, but not fast enough. The
fireplace belched a massive cloud of black soot into
the room. Everything was drenched in a blanket of
fine black dust; the white tinsel, the peace letters, the
white tree, even Tracey.

But she'd no time to assess the damage.

The sooty crow flapped from one end of the living
room to the other in a mad panic. It mapped out a
pattern of black and grey splodges as it battered itself
against the ceiling in an attempt to escape a crazed
Wolfie.

The dog bayed, yelped and jumped up, nearly

catching the bird. Wolfie knocked the Christmas tree over. Tracey stood momentarily frozen, unable to decide which direction to run as the crow and the dog scrambled back and forth through the living room.

On the next pass, she grabbed the dog. Tommy ran in from the backyard, shouting at Wolfie to be quiet. He dashed to the window and flung it wide open. But the crow was at the far end of the room beating itself against the French doors into the kitchen. Tommy darted towards it. He tried to grab the bird but sprang back as the crow pecked lumps out of his hands. It decided to make another dash for the bay window, appearing to fear Wolfie's chaotic barking less than the waving human. Tommy followed the bird, corralling it in the right direction. He pushed past Tracey and Wolfie when the dog wriggled out of Tracey's hands. Tommy tripped over Wolfie and crashed face-first against the coffee table. His feet tangled with Tracey's, and she lost her balance.

She landed on top of Tommy. Her nose met his elbow with a skull shuddering impact. Pain exploded in her face from her teeth to her forehead and all the way to each ear. A spear of nausea made her retch in one violent hiccup, but she didn't vomit.

The crow climbed out the window and flew off.

She crawled backwards off Tommy, protecting her nose with one hand and warding off the dog's wet tongue with the other hand. Tommy rolled over slowly, groaning and cursing. As he sat up, Tracey saw blood pouring from his lips down his chin.

"Shit! Are you okay?" she asked, alarmed. Did he have some kind of internal injury?

"Oh, God, are *you* okay?" He crawled to her.

His distress scared her. Was her nose that badly broken? With the pain she felt, it could be sideways on her face.

"It's just a buthed lip," he said. "You?"

"Bust dose," she answered. "Is it crooked?"

"No, I don't fink is broken." He peered at her closely, giving her a close up of his split lip. A paper stitch would fix that.

"What the fuck happ'ed?" she asked, looking around her at the carnage in the room. The tree was on its side, the lights still on, and everything was covered in black dust. A rubble of soot, twigs and feathers lay in the fireplace and spread outwards into the room.

"I juss wan'ed to do som-fing 'pecial," Tommy said. "When the chimney sweep was here, I used his ladder to set up the present so it would fall down the chimney when I released the string I'd tied in the yard. He'd already dropped a stone down, and it was fine. The crow fucked it all up!"

"Something special? Da only something special I wan'ed was for you to try to ged along with Dermot. You didn't listen to me. You're so dam stubborn and now look at us?" Tracey said.

Tommy bent forward, reaching for the black bag poking out of a pile of soot and twigs. The simple gesture fuelled her irritation with him. She knew he was trying to make this special, but he wasn't listening to her.

"Just leave it there!" she snapped.

His arm recoiled as if the present were hot. He looked at it. Tracey could tell it was killing him to do nothing, and it gave her bitter satisfaction. Let him stew.

27

But then she felt sorry for him and geared up to apologise.

"In fairness, this would have happened even if Dermot was coming over tomorrow," Tommy mumbled.

"Oh, shut up!" Tracey said, her compassion sublimating to fury. He was so fucking stubborn. She stormed to the side table and snatched a fistful of tissues from the box. "You fucked up, Tommy. Not because you filled the house with soot and nearly broke my nose, no because you denied me the one thing I wanted for Christmas. And I gave you everything you asked for. Dinner with Aileen, dinner with your dad, though in fairness, I don't mind that," she added in a mumble. She dabbed at her nose. "Fuck!" she shouted as much at herself as at him. "There I go again, making you feel better. Christ All-fucking-mighty."

Tommy winced. "Okay, I get it."

"Do you?" she asked, still furious. "Really? You promised to try six weeks ago, but you haven't tried at all."

Tommy took a deep breath and said. "You're right. I'm sorry. First, I was so bitter. We'd just buried Molly. I put it off. Now it's awkward. I don't know where to start."

"Start here, start tomorrow. I'm not asking you to be what you guys once were. Just be civil in each other's company. Dermot's changed, really changed. He's devoted to Cara and not because she's Sheila's baby, but because she's his daughter."

They fell silent. Tracey's mind swung like a trapeze artist from one "if only" to the next, each one painful and fruitless. No one could wind back the clock. Cara was not Molly's baby. They had to deal with reality.

"Text him. Invite him," Tommy said. "I'll try. I promise."

Tracey delicately hugged Tommy and murmured in his ear, "Thank you, best gift ever."

Christmas Day

Tracey woke up with a throbbing headache and two black eyes. Her nose was not broken, and the bleeding had stopped soon after the injury. Tommy's bottom lip, swollen to twice its size, was capped by a black clot held in place with paper stitches from their first aid kit.

Tracy prepared the potatoes, carrots, parsnips and Brussel sprouts as the roasting gammon joint and turkey filled the kitchen with the rich aroma of Christmas dinner. This was the first year she'd hosted and had bought far too much food, even with the last-minute additions of Sean and Dermot.

Christmas music played on the kitchen radio, but the sound was soon drowned out by Tommy vacuuming the living room in an attempt to set the room to rights. The tinsel and the white tree had turned a drab shade of grey. With the lights on, it looked … well, too late now. They'd have to push on through

"A man on a galloping horse wouldn't notice," Tommy declared.

"Don't mention galloping animals in the living room, please," Tracey answered.

"Don't make me smile," Tommy said, touching his fingertips to his bust lip. "It hurts too much."

Dermot arrived first. He stood at the door, clutching the baby carrier and stared at the spectacle in front of him. He didn't look much better. Cara had kept him up for two nights straight. Red rimmed eyelids gave way to mauve tinged skin, grey where the inner eyes met his nose. At least he had an excuse for looking crap, Tracey thought.

"What…are…is everything okay with you guys?" Dermot asked.

"Yes, we tripped over the dog," Tommy said, reaching for the baby carrier. "Please, come in."

"She's sleeping, at last," Dermot said, his voice hushed. "Don't swing her too much—"

"I know how to carry a baby." Tommy glared at Dermot

"I know you do. Sorry. Tracey says you're great with her. Thanks." Dermot's voice was steeped with exhaustion.

"Don't mention it," Tommy mumbled, and Tracey noticed flames in his cheeks. She hoped he was embarrassed at snapping at Dermot and not plain angry. His closed face made it hard for her to read Tommy as he settled Cara's carrier on an armchair before going out the back to bring in Wolfie.

Dermot tugged Tracey's arm and said in her ear, "Seriously, did he do this to you? Because if —"

"No!" Tracey exclaimed. "Jesus, you know him.

It's the same old Tommy, and if you want to patch things up, this is not the way. Now, sit yourself there and behave."

Dermot sloughed off his coat and sat down on the sofa. Wolfie came in and sniffed the baby carrier.

"Here, boy," Dermot called him away from Cara. Wolfie sat by Dermot and dunted his snout under his hand, heaving a contented sigh as Dermot automatically complied with petting him.

Tracey left him while she checked on food and found Tommy stocking up the beer in the fridge.

"Will you bring one of those in to Dermot?" she asked.

"Don't leave me on my own in there," Tommy said.

She raised an eyebrow.

"Okay, okay," He rummaged in the back of the fridge and found a cold beer, popped the lid and moved towards the living room.

"Would you look," Tommy whispered to Tracey. "Fatherhood is taking its toll. He's committed to that wee pet. I'll give him that."

Dermot sat on the sofa, head back, snoring softly. Wolfie lay stretched along the sofa, his head in Dermot's lap, fast asleep. Still strapped into the baby carrier on the chair beside the tree, the baby examined her hands like they were the most wonderful discovery ever.

Tommy saw his dad's car pull up outside. Wolfie heard it too and jumped up, barking. The baby started crying. Dermot woke up, and Tracey thought for a second he might join in.

"Wolfie, Kitchen," Tommy commanded. The dog slunk off, and Tommy closed him in.

Dermot picked Cara up, and she soothed immediately. Tracey answered the door.

"Oh, my God!" Carmel said. "What the hell happened to you? You're like a throwback to the eighties with all that pink and purple 'round your eyes."

"Nice to see you, Mum." Tracey bent forward and kissed her on the cheek. "Happy Christmas, Sean." She gave Tommy's dad a hug and air kiss.

Tommy appeared at her side.

"Jaysus Christ! Were you two fighting?" Carmel asked.

"No!" Tommy and Tracey said together.

"Come on in, and we'll tell you *all* about it." Tracey led the way to the living room.

She felt an unexpected thrill when she heard her mother exclaim with joy, "Ach son, I wasn't expecting to see you. And there's our Cara. Give her here?"

Tracey watched them embrace and fuss over the baby. It felt good. She smiled at Tommy, and he winked.

Sean cleared his throat and said, "So what's the craic? What happened to you guys, were you attacked?"

A replication of his father, Tommy also cleared his throat. "In a manner of speaking – you see, here's what I was trying to do…"

He went on to tell them that he had hung a present for Tracey inside the chimney with the intention of dropping it on Christmas Eve but that the plan had gone pear-shaped when he'd flushed the crow down the chimney.

At that part, Carmel said, "Oh no, a bird in the house! That's terrible bad luck, you know."

"You're telling me," Tracey said.

"Well, next thing," Tommy said. "There's soot everywhere, the bird's flying up and down. The dog's going ballistic trying to catch it. I tripped over the dog and smacked my lip off the edge of the coffee table."

"Ow," Carmel and Dermot said as Sean sucked air in past his teeth.

"Then I tripped over Tommy and hit my nose off his elbow," Tracey said. "And we're all lying in a soot-covered, bloody heap, and the bird just flies out the window."

Carmel started to chuckle first. Dermot struggled for a few seconds to keep his face straight but gave in. When Sean began to crack, Tracey piped up, "It's not funny."

"Unfortunately, it is," Tommy said woefully. "But please, Tracey, don't you dare laugh. If you laugh, I'll laugh." He pinched his fingers around the wound on his lips. "And if I laugh, this cut opens again. Dammit."

"So what about the present?" Carmel asked.

"The moment was kind of lost," Tommy said. "But I retrieved it."

He pulled a small, black velvet bag from a drawer in the sideboard.

"Happy Christmas, Tracey."

She opened the bag and pulled out a flat white jewellery box with Pandora written on it. She gasped. "Is it…?" she asked, grinning.

"I've seen you admiring these.' Tommy touched his nose. "Not much gets past me."

She opened the box, and there lay a shiny charm bracelet.

"It's not full yet, but we'll add to it. Each charm

34

represents someone in your life. That's me." Tommy pointed to a jewelled heart with the word "Love" in gold. Colour rose in his cheeks.

"Oh look, there's 'daughter'!" Carmel pointed at another charm with a heart-shaped, pink crystal.

"Maybe someday that will represent me too," Sean said with a wink.

"I love it," Tracey breathed. "It has a sister charm." She looked up at Dermot. "And auntie, see?" she said, holding it up in front of Cara's face. Cara blew a raspberry. They all laughed.

"Thanks for that, Tommy," Dermot said.

"Of course, you're family," Tommy said.

Tracey caught the look they exchanged, a fragile peace offering, the gossamer beginning of reconciliation. It couldn't, wouldn't happen all at once. She had to be patient. Giving them space for their moment, she looked down at her bracelet again.

"Oh, look – now that's hilarious!" Tracey pointed to a squat little silver charm in the shape of a dog's head that said "devoted dog."

She looked at the next one, and her eyes filled with tears. Welcome tears in a strange way, for the charm was a little angel, and suddenly she felt Molly's humour fill her with a warmth she hadn't felt in a long time. "Oh my God," she whispered. "It makes the hiking boots I got you really boring! But it's perfect."

"Of course, it's perfect. It represents you," Tommy took her hand. "Because you are what links us all together and makes us a family."

"Thank you." Tracey hugged him, then pulled away and saw the wetness in Dermot's eyes too.

"Okay, before I start crying, let's get everyone

35

together and take a photo for Cara's first Christmas." Tracey lifted the camera off the sideboard and set up the self-timer. "Tommy, grab the dog so I don't trip over him."

They posed several times until they had a shot of everyone looking at the camera, baby and dog included.

"That was quite the operation!" Dermot said as they settled back into chairs.

"Let's see it again," Carmel said. Tracey passed her the camera. "Good grief, what a motley looking crew."

"Yep." Tracey looked at the picture. "But we'll certainly all remember Cara's first Christmas."

"Except maybe, Cara," Tommy said, snuggling the baby and warding off the dog's slobbering advances. "Right enough, look at the state of us."

Tracey started laughing, thinking about something Orla had said.

"Well," she said, holding up the photo. "There's always Photoshop."

The End

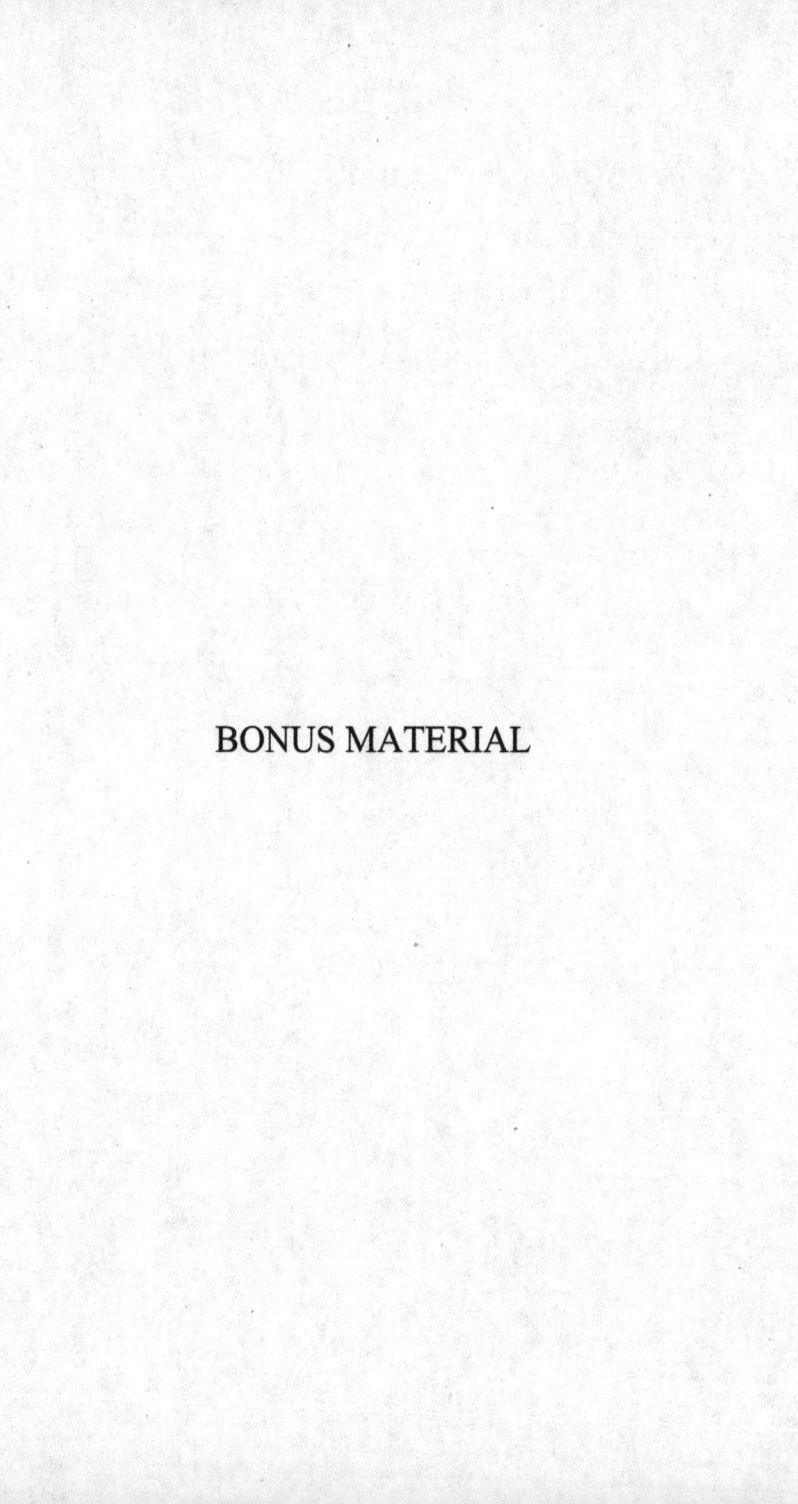

BONUS MATERIAL

How Irish Legends Inspired A Science Fiction Trilogy About Getting Younger.

An Article by Byddi Lee

As I was growing up, the Irish legends that captured my imagination most were not the daring-does of Cuchulainn – The Hound of Ulster nor the stories of Macha – the queen who gave her name to my home town Armagh. In fact, the ancient warriors and royalty didn't interest me at all, but those stories that involved distorted ageing and extended longevity did. It was an indulgence of sorts to weave the essence of these stories into *The Rejuvenation Trilogy*.

Rejuvenation is set in a dystopian future. There are matter streamers to provide food, hovercrafts for transportation, and carebots to tend to the frail. Against this backdrop of technology, we see a society that is top-heavy with an aged population. People still yearn to be and stay young.

The Irish fairy tales have stood the test of time and inspire the children of that era, such as our main characters, Bobbie and Gracie, fraternal twins. Gracie suffers from a rapid ageing disease called Progeria and is particularly drawn to the stories of

Tír na nÓg, the Land of the Forever Young that's far across the waves and can only be reached by a magic horse, as she explains to Bobbie…

"'I'm no angel," Gracie said, grinning. "I'm one of the little people, a leprechaun! And I'm going to escape to Tír na nÓg."

"To where?" Bobbie asked.

"The land of everlasting youth. Everyone is beautiful and young there, and when I go there, I'll look just like you," Gracie said. "But with black hair, like Daddy."

"How do you know all this?"

"I read about it on the Internet."

"Can I come?" Bobbie couldn't imagine being anywhere without Gracie.

"Yes, but you'll have to wait until when you're old. Like me." Gracie's fuchsia pink dress reflected off her skin, giving her bare, veined scalp an ethereal glow.

"But you're only nine. We're the same age."

"Yes, but I'm the one who's a fairy, remember? I'll watch over you from Tír na nÓg. Time passes slower there than it does in Armagh, so it will only feel like ten minutes to me before you're there, too.'"

Excerpt from *Rejuvenation Book 1*

The Children of Lir is another legend that tells of excessive ageing and longevity. Lir's children are turned into swans by their stepmother and sent into exile for three hundred years. They returned to their home in Ireland and resumed human form

2

– as three-hundred year-old humans – then died. I'm grossly paraphrasing, but nonetheless, it's a tragic tale.

We find out early in *Rejuvenation Book 1* that Gracie died from her condition at the age of 13. Her death left a lasting effect on her twin sister Bobbie who, feeling she had acquired a unique understanding of ageing because of Gracie, went on to become a geriatrician. In *Rejuvenation Book 2,* Bobbie uses the fairy tale of the *Children of Lir* to make sense of ageing and death in the real world, a challenge for her since she sees both daily in her job.

Other Irish fairy tales hold more promise, like the one about Fionn Mc Cool being tricked by the old witch, the Calliagh Berra on top of Slieve Gullion, the highest mountain in County Armagh. As the story goes, one day, Fionn found a young woman crying by the lake at the top of the mountain. When he asked her why she said she'd dropped her gold ring into the lake. Being the hero he was, he jumped in after it. But the girl was the old witch who was jealous of her sister for being in love with Fionn. The witch had put a spell on the lake so that when Fionn came out, he had aged to become a

3

withered old man with white hair. But Fionn's followers made the witch reverse the spell, and he became young again.

The *Rejuvenation Trilogy* is all about regaining lost youth and its consequences. Bobbie's most elderly patients contract a strange disease which proves fatal to some but others, including her Granny, survive and become younger, fitter and psychopathic!

I was drawn to the idea that eternal youth wasn't exactly the be-all and end-all and wanted to explore the gifts that come with age. In a society that values the beauty of youth, that's quite a challenge, but even the Irish legends will have us realise that the beauty of youth is only skin deep, as in the story of Oisin, Fionn Mc Cool's son.

As the story goes, Oisín falls in love with Niamh, a woman of the Otherworld. She takes him across the waves on a magic horse to Tír na nÓg. After what feels like three years to Oisín, he becomes homesick and wants to return to Ireland. Niamh warns him to stay on the magic horse and never touch the ground. But when Oisín returns, he discovers that 300 years have passed in Ireland. He falls from the horse and instantly ages. As the years catch up with him, he quickly dies.

In *Rejuvenation Book 1,* this same legend is reflected in several instances of age catching up quickly on a youthful body. Although this legend is not actually recounted, it forms the basis of some of Bobbie's nightmares.

'By the time Death carried Gracie to Tír na nÓg four years later, Bobbie had read scores of legends about the Land of the Forever Young. Alone in the bedroom Bobbie had once shared with Gracie, she'd jolt awake after dreaming of her twin sister returning for her on a white horse, young and beautiful, her black hair billowing out behind her. Bobbie would reach for Gracie, but as their hands touched, Gracie's hair would turn white, her skin would wrinkle, her body crumple as she died all over again from old age.'
Excerpt from *Rejuvenation Book*

Ultimately, the idea of folding the old fairy tales into a high-tech dystopian future is a metaphor for life – we can't forge ahead and embrace the new and the vivacious unless we can carry with us and learn from the stories and wisdom from years gone by.

Byddi Lee

REJUVENATION BOOK 1

The *Melter War* has left the earth's surface devastated, leaving humanity to survive on what little land is left between the Scorch Zones and the rising oceans, where towering subscrapers dot the dystopian shorelines.

Bobbie Chan is a doctor caring for the ultra-elderly in one such subscraper when she notices a mysterious, new disease afflicting her patients; some show signs of age reversal before a catastrophic, and often fatal, cardiac arrest strikes.

Bobbie begins to wonder if she is witnessing a bioweapon in full force. A Melter attack? Are they destined to finish the war they started?

Belus Corp, the 'saviour' of humanity during the Melter War, whisk the afflicted away; including Bobbie's grandmother. But Bobbie is terrified. The 'Rejuvenees' are getting younger, but they are also becoming increasingly aggressive, uncontrollably so.

Bobbie begins a race against time to rescue the Rejuvenees and uncover their true enemy.

REJUVENATION BOOK 2

Is Rejuvenation really humanity's saviour, or is it the hidden doorway to slavery and persecution?

Bobbie Chan has escaped the clutches of the all-encompassing Belus Corporation. She and her comrades are forced to seek sanctuary amongst a band of renegades - outcasts who eke out a meagre existence in the barren wastelands that emerged from the Melter War.

However, Bobbie finds herself at the heart of a game plan devised by the renegades to bring the Belus Corporation to its knees.

This second instalment of the Rejuvenation Trilogy sees old friends becoming enemies and one-time enemies becoming friends as the true, diabolical nature of Rejuvenation becomes clear.

REJUVENATION BOOK 3

Out of a clear, blue sky, a mysterious alien race wreaked havoc on planet Earth, thus beginning the Melter War.

Alien energy weapons struck the Polar ice caps. Oceans rose, drowned huge swathes of land, swallowed up great cities and left much of the earth as an irradiated wasteland. Millions of people died.

But a saviour emerged; Lisette Fox and her Belus Corporation supplied the weapons and technology to defeat the Melters and brought peace back to the world.

Some two decades later, Bobbie Chan, a child at the outbreak of war, now works as a doctor caring for the ultra-elderly. Bobbie encounters a previously unidentified disease, 'Rejuvenation', which makes the old young but has homicidal side effects.

In this gripping final instalment of Byddi Lee's Rejuvenation Trilogy, Bobbie discovers the shocking truth behind the Melter's attack and Rejuvenation. Bobbie faces a decision with untold consequences, not only for Bobbie but for the entire human race.

MARCH TO NOVEMBER

Five people and eight months. A broken marriage, an arson attack, a death, a birth and a psychotic break.

March to November navigates the entangled lives of Tracey Duggan and her circle of friends and foes in modern-day Belfast, Ireland, as they struggle with love, lust, loyalty and betrayal.

All Tracey wants is a normal life with a nice guy. All she has, however, is a violent ex-boyfriend intent upon making her life hell.

Can Tracey have a normal relationship? Will her new boyfriend Tommy get the acceptance from his father that he craves? Will her sister-in-law Molly get over her cheating husband, Dermot? Can Dermot's bitch lover Sheila really have it all?

Modern Day Belfast is not the city of bombs and bullets of their childhood, but life is still full of trouble for these five as they alternately walk, run and stumble along the road toward a finale that is both heart-breaking and freeing.

THE BRAMLEY – VOLUMES 1 & 2 ANTHOLOGIES OF FLASH FICTION ARMAGH

Edited by Byddi Lee and Réamonn Ó Ciaráin

The Bramley is a collection of Flash Fiction stories that cover an eclectic range of genre and subject. This diversity ensures something for everyone. Like a good Armagh Bramley apple, this collection is sharp yet tasty, combining bitter with sweet to tantalise and awaken the literary palate.

A BRAMLEY TASTER

Beheaded

By Byddi Lee

I recognise your face right away. A year ago, your beard might have thrown me off but not now. It's impossible to shave when you can barely move. The neck brace gets in the way, but I dare not remove it. I ignore the itching. Scratching is a gamble – one wrong move, never move again.

Silence enfolds us, drifting with the dust motes, as we face each other in this temporary exhibition in the Armagh County Museum. Damp sounds of traffic slosh in from outside. A muffled cough. A parent hisses urgent whispers to the quick footfalls of a child running where it shouldn't. We hold our tranquillity, united by it, comfortable with it.

I stare. Hardly believing what I see but unable to deny it, your face, there behind the glass, echoes my face.

Do you know me?

Of course, you don't. But I know you.

How am I familiar with *your* face when my wife is a stranger to me, my kids are aliens, and my parents could be any of the people I see on the street?

Yet, I know you.

The accident snuffed out my memory, a candle flame between damp finger and thumb. My head is as empty as your skull, you poor sod. My past is a blank screen, all channels off-air, except the one showing the flickering image of broken ice in a muddy pothole and a narrow bicycle wheel spinning to the burr of car horns.

I know you, despite the years, the centuries, the millennia that separate us, regardless of the impossibility of you turning up here and me seeing you here. I see your face every day, but usually, it looks at me from the bathroom mirror. It's the only place I take time to study it, puzzled, inquisitive and much more animated than right now – but it's the same face always searching mine – always asking the same questions. Who are you? What happened to you? And, now I've found *you*, I ask you the same questions. Who are you? What happened to you?

I see your injuries, the same as mine, almost.

I read the museum blurb about you. Someone smashed your head, cut it off and threw it in a ditch where it sat for a thousand years. Now, your skull is finally found, but no one understands you – except me, because you could *be* me.

Did the fracture on your skull whip away your memory too?

No, it ended your life. No induced coma for you. No medication to reduce the swelling of your brain. Your injury was not an accident but a deliberate swing of a weapon, a sword. No brace for your neck.

Where did our memories go?

The woman who says she's my wife interrupts us.

'What's up?' she says, flashing that smile – her way of non-verbally telling me, 'I'm your wife even if you don't remember me.'

But that smile inexplicably raises my hackles.

I'm ashamed of my gut reaction, my anger at her. But if she knows me like she says she does, she'd stop pushing me to remember when I clearly cannot.

Yet, she deserves an effort on my part.

'Look at the facial reconstruction of the skull,' I say, and I point to you.

She hooks her wrist around my elbow and leans in. Her hair falls forward as she peers at you. All I see is the tip of her nose and chin. She unhooks her hand from my elbow and slides long-nailed fingers through her hair, tucking it behind her ear as she cocks her head, looking from you to me.

Maybe it's the bow of her lips stretching straight or the dimple puckering her cheek, or simply the wonderment as she says, 'Oh my goodness! He looks just like you!'

A memory slams into my head, the screen blasts on in vivid Technicolor.

She's looking at our baby boy, just born and saying the same words.

And I remember! I *remember* that first staggering sense of love, protectiveness and tenderness for our child, hers and mine.

More pictures, thoughts, memories unfurl and carpet my mind.

The first moment I met my wife and life blossomed with longing and love.

The coffin my father was laid to rest in and the drag of his loss.

My sister making me laugh like no one else can, making my beautiful kids laugh the same way.

My mother's perfume – the scent of comfort,

3

home.

Like old friends, my memories repopulate, and the files on the people I `love, replenish.

You smile.

I turn, do a double-take before realising that it's my reflection on the glass overlaid on your face that's smiling.

'Maybe he's your ancestor," she says.

'Perhaps.'

I hook my little finger around hers – our special way of holding hands.

Her eyes widen.

She knows.

I know.

The End

ABOUT THE AUTHOR

Byddi Lee is the author of "Rejuvenation," a speculative fiction trilogy and has published flash fiction, short stories and her novel, "March to November." Byddi co-founded and manages Flash Fiction Armagh, shortlisted as Best Regular Spoken Word Night in the Saboteur Awards and co-edited "The Bramley – An Anthology of Flash Fiction Armagh" Volumes 1 and 2. Byddi co-wrote the play "IMPACT – Armagh's Train Disaster", staged for the anniversary of the tragedy in June 2019 in the Abbey Lane Theatre in Armagh. She co-wrote "Zoomeo & Juliet" and "Social Bubble, Toil & Trouble" – live plays performed on Zoom by the Armagh Theatre during the lockdown. Byddi is grateful to be an Arts Council Northern Ireland supported writer and holds professional membership at the Irish Writers Centre in Dublin.

For more information, check out her website www.byddilee.com
Or follow her on Twitter @Byddi